GRANDMA'S

written by MALKA DRUCKER

illustrated by EVE CHWAST

HARCOURT BRACE JOVANOVICH, PUBLISHERS

San Diego New York London

LATKES

Thanks to my sister, Pam, for inspiring me with this idea
— M. D.

Requests for permission to make copies of any part
of the work should be mailed to: Permissions Department,
Harcourt Brace Jovanovich, Publishers, 8th Floor,
Orlando, Florida 32887.

Library of Congress Cataloging-in-Publication Data
Drucker, Malka.
Grandma's latkes/by Malka Drucker; illustrated by Eve Chwast. —
1st ed.
p.   cm.
"Gulliver books."
Summary: Grandma explains the meaning of Hanukkah while showing
Molly how to cook latkes for the holiday.
ISBN 0-15-200468-8
[1. Hanukkah — Fiction. 2. Hanukkah cookery — Fiction. 3. Cookery,
Jewish — Fiction. 4. Jews — Fiction.] I. Chwast, Eve, ill.
II. Title.
PZ7.D824Gr   1992
[E] — dc20   91-30086

First edition
A B C D E

The illustrations in this book are woodcuts
printed on Japanese rice paper and painted with watercolor.
The text type was set in Cochin by Thompson Type, San Diego, California.
Color separations were made by Bright Arts, Ltd., Singapore.
Printed and bound by Tien Wah Press, Singapore
Production supervision by Warren Wallerstein and Ginger Boyer
Designed by Lisa Peters

For Grandma Mae and Grandma Rae
— M. D.

For my sister, Pam
— E. C.

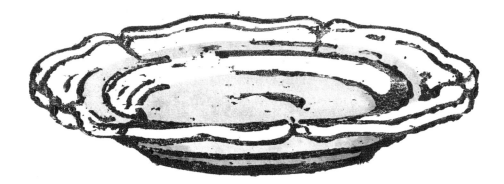

No matter how Molly tried, she could never beat Grandma at grating potatoes. One potato after another flew from Grandma's hands into a mountain of slippery white slivers.

"How did you learn to make latkes?" Molly asked. She rested her tired arms but didn't complain. She was finally old enough to be picked as Grandma's helper. They had lots of latkes to make for the Hanukkah party.

"From *my* grandmother. Before Hanukkah, she would save her pennies —
she was very poor — to buy potatoes, eggs, onions, and oil. All of us — you
remember, I have five brothers and sisters — would be in the kitchen when she
fried the latkes. Look at my recipe. It's in her handwriting. She used three
potatoes, but we'll use six because we have so many people."

Grandma put the potatoes in a bowl and took out the eggs, onions, salt, and pepper.

"Why do we eat latkes during Hanukkah? Is it because Jews ate them a long time ago?" Molly asked.

"No. It's because it reminds us of the oil. Take out the oil, Molly, while we're talking." As Molly went to the pantry, Grandma began to grate the onions. Tears rolled down her cheeks. "It's just the onions," she told Molly, smiling.

Molly asked, "How do you know how many onions to use?"

"Well, look. My grandma wrote, 'Use one onion for three potatoes.' Do you know the story of Hanukkah?"

"Not really."

"Well, why don't you break the eggs into this bowl, and I'll tell it to you. A long time ago, Jews did eat potatoes, but they also ate lots of other vegetables and fruits, because they were farmers in Israel.

They lived plain, simple lives, and they were happy raising families and celebrating the holidays."

"But they didn't have Hanukkah yet?"

"That's right. The trouble began when Antiochus, the Syrian king, became ruler of Israel and demanded that everyone pray to Greek gods. No other religion was allowed."

"That would be like everyone having to celebrate Christmas," Molly said. "No more Hanukkah and latkes. I don't think I like Antiochus." She broke the first egg into the bowl.

"Many people didn't," Grandma answered.

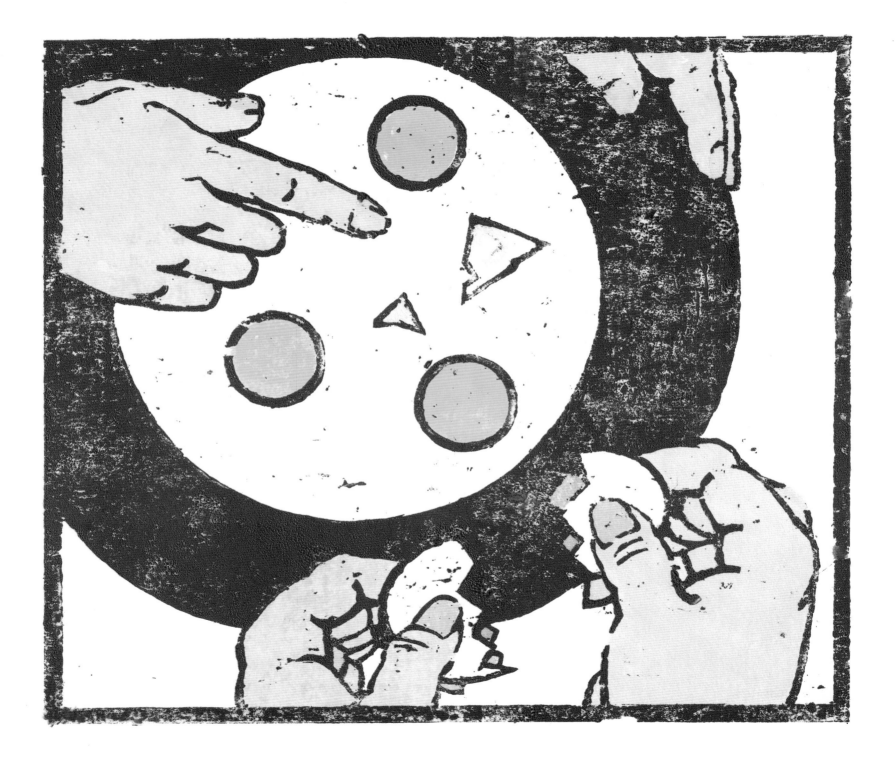

"Uh-oh, Grandma! Part of the eggshell fell into the eggs, and I can't get it out! It keeps jumping away from me." Molly's fingers dripped with sticky egg whites. No matter what she tried, she couldn't get hold of the shell.

"Watch this," Grandma said. She dipped another piece of eggshell into the bowl, and out came the piece Molly had dropped.

"Let me try that," Molly said, and Grandma threw in another bit of shell. Like Grandma, Molly easily fished out the eggshell with the piece in her hand. "I like that trick!"

"Good." Grandma smiled. "Now mix the potatoes, onions, and eggs together, Molly." Grandma poured oil into the big frying pan and turned on the stove.

"So did the Jewish people get mad at Antiochus?" Molly continued.

"Yes, eventually. One day Antiochus sent a soldier to Mattathias, a wise old man who lived near Jerusalem. The soldier said, 'Antiochus will make you rich and powerful if you help him. Just kill this pig and eat a little of it. Then all the Jews will follow your example.' You know, Molly, in those days, no Jews ate meat from a pig.

"But Mattathias screamed at the soldier, 'Go away! Don't tell me what to eat or who to believe in!'

"Suddenly a grubby little man who had been listening stepped forward. 'I'll eat the meat,' he whispered.

"This made Mattathias very angry. He couldn't understand how someone would throw away his religion so easily. So he killed both the man and the soldier and shouted, 'All who believe in God, follow me!'"

Molly stopped stirring the mixture and stared at Grandma. "So did they?" she asked.

"Well, some did," Grandma answered.

She sprinkled some salt and pepper into the bowl and said, "Now we're ready to fry the latkes. First we take a tablespoon of the mixture and drop the spoonful into the hot bubbly oil." Grandma made eight circles in the frying pan, and they sizzled and turned brown. Molly's mouth began to water.

Grandma picked her up to watch the latkes fry. "Don't put your face too close. My grandmother would say, 'Stand back! The oil jumps out! You'll get burned!' But we wouldn't go far, because we couldn't wait to eat her crispy hot latkes."

When the oil had stopped spitting, Grandma went on with the story. "Mattathias had five sons. The oldest was Judah Maccabee. Judah and his brothers led a small army against Antiochus and his huge army of thousands of soldiers. And guess what, Molly? A miracle happened. The Maccabees won."

"How could the Maccabees win?" Molly asked.

"Well, no one knows for sure how a miracle happens — it's a mystery.
But Judah Maccabee knew his little country very well and surprised
Antiochus by hiding in the hills. And they knew they had to win.

If they didn't, the Jewish people would be destroyed. But mostly, they felt they had the spirit of God inside them, and that gave them strength.

"The Maccabees returned to their big, beautiful Temple in Jerusalem, ready to celebrate. Instead, they cried. The Temple was filthy — blood, dirt, and ashes covered everything. All the books, Torahs, and candlesticks were gone.

"Worst of all, when Judah tried to light the menorah, there was only a drop of oil. That was only enough for maybe one day. But when oil was poured into the lamp it burned for a second day, and a third. In all it burned for eight days!"

"How did that happen?" asked Molly.

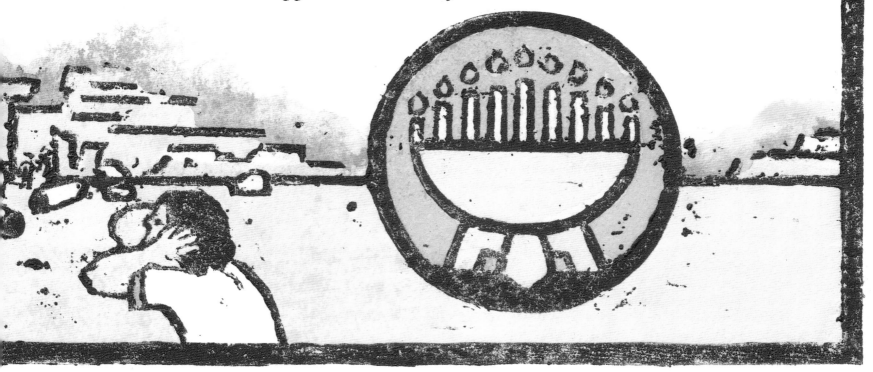

"It was another miracle, just like the Maccabees beating Antiochus, and just like you, Molly. You're my miracle." Grandma wrapped a latke in a paper towel and handed it to Molly. Molly bit into the hot crisp pancake and sighed with pleasure. Grandma brought a big plate covered with a paper towel over to the frying pan. "So that's why on Hanukkah we fry latkes in lots of oil."

"And eat them."

"You bet. Help me put the latkes on the plate." She lifted them out of the pan with a spatula and drained them on the paper towel.

When they were finally ready, Molly and Grandma carried in the heavy platter of golden pancakes to the rest of the family who were waiting at the table. "Mm — delicious," Grandpa said as he smeared sour cream over his latke.

Molly's mother said, "I heard you and Grandma talking the whole time you were cooking. What was going on?"

Molly answered, "I learned lots of things. Cooking secrets."

"Like what?"

"How to fish eggshell out of a bowl of eggs," Molly said. "The next time we cook, I'll show you."

"Good. What else did you learn?" Molly's mother asked.

Molly swallowed a bite of applesauce-covered latke and said, "I learned a lot. About how Judah Maccabee beat Antiochus, even though Antiochus was much stronger. And how a tiny drop of oil lasted for eight days. Those were miracles, and Hanukkah is about miracles." She thought a moment. "Grandma, do we light candles for eight nights because the light lasted eight days?"

Grandma laughed and said, "Exactly. Now you know enough to teach your own grandchildren," and she gave Molly a kiss.

Grandma's Latkes

Invite an adult to help you make these latkes.

This is Grandma's recipe, which calls for grating the potatoes by hand. You can follow her old-fashioned way, or grate the potatoes in a food processor.

3 large potatoes
1 small onion
2 beaten eggs
2 tablespoons flour
1 teaspoon salt
pinch of pepper
½ cup vegetable oil

Wash the potatoes very well, but don't peel them. Grate them coarsely into a bowl. Grate in the onion. Add the beaten eggs, flour, salt, and pepper. Let the mixture sit for ten minutes to thicken. Pour off excess liquid. Heat the vegetable oil for one minute in a frying pan, then drop tablespoonfuls of the mixture into the pan. When the pancakes are brown around the edges, turn and fry them until the other sides are crispy. Drain them on paper towels, and eat them with sour cream and applesauce.